T0368993

Never Look Back

Nancy Byrne

Illustrated by Nader Batayeh

Balboa Press books may be ordered through booksellers or by contacting:

Balboa Press
A Division of Hay House
1663 Liberty Drive
Bloomington, IN 47403
www.balboapress.com
844-682-1282

ISBN: 978-1-9822-6720-9 (sc)
ISBN: 978-1-9822-6718-6 (hc)
ISBN: 978-1-9822-6719-3 (e)

Library of Congress Control Number: 2021907296

Print information available on the last page.

Balboa Press rev. date: 04/13/2021

BALBOA.PRESS
A DIVISION OF HAY HOUSE

Dedication

This book is dedicated to all of my Soul Sisters. They have supported me through thick and thin.
I have many.

Soul Sister

noun

1: one who provides the most joy and strength

2: best kind of friend who always feels like home

3: kindred spirit

4: chosen family

And to my teacher/friend Nader.

Thank you for sharing your love of art . . . It's contagious!

Inspired by Al Hirschfeld, an American caricature artist, Nader has cleverly hidden the name 'ELLIE' somewhere in each of the illustrations.

How many 'ELLIE's' can you find?

Ellie was one happy girl. She, along with her sister Bonnie, lived on a farm with Dr. Michael. He was a kind man who lived a quiet life on a quiet farm. He cared for all kinds of animals and loved them all, but Ellie held a special place in his heart.

Ellie was adopted by Dr. Michael at a time when she needed him most. Ellie loved Dr. Michael, or "Doc" as she liked to call him. Ellie loved her sister Bonnie. Ellie loved everyone she met. She never had a mean thing to say about anyone.

But, not everyone that Ellie met felt the same. You see, Ellie was, shall we say, a plump girl. . .well, a chubby girl. . .well, let's just say she was well-rounded.

Sadly, Ellie's nickname among many of her peers was Ellie, Ellie, Big Fat Belly. Sometimes they would even say it to her face!

Every time Ellie walked past them, she heard. . ."Ellie, Ellie, Big Fat Belly," and every time, Ellie held her head high and said, "Never look back." Confused, they would turn their heads and look behind them.

They wondered what Ellie meant.

Every night Dr. Michael would
tuck Ellie & Bonnie into their
bed. He would kiss them
gently on the forehead and tell
them that he loved them.

Ellie and Bonnie were not only sisters, they were also best friends.

Bedtime was one of their favorite times because that's when Ellie and her big sister would talk about the day. One night Ellie was quiet. Bonnie asked Ellie to tell her what was on her mind. Ellie sighed and asked, "Why do the words, 'Never Look Back' hold such a special place in my heart?"

Bonnie was quiet for a moment.
She thought back to a time when
she was teased about her eye.
Then she said, "I think it's time
you asked Doc that question."

The next morning Ellie asked Dr. Michael, "Why is it, that whenever I'm teased by others, the words 'Never Look Back' come to mind?" With tears in his eyes, Dr. Michael said, "I guess it's time to tell you about the day you came to me, Ellie."

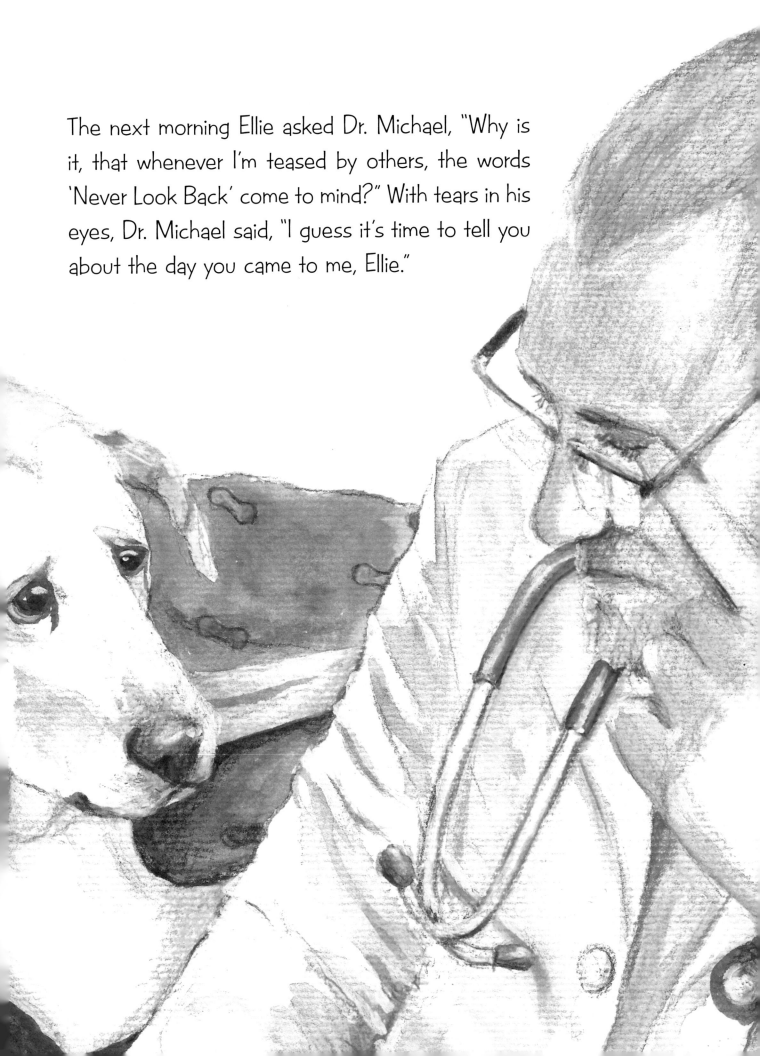

Dr. Michael left the table where they sat and brought back a yellow envelope. Inside the envelope was a picture. Ellie looked at it, looked at Dr. Michael, and then looked at it again. With her head tilted in confusion, she asked, "Who is that?"

Dr. Michael looked into Ellie's sweet eyes and answered, "That is you. That was you the day that you became mine." Ellie remained quiet. How could the dog in the picture be her? This dog was skin and bones and looked nothing like the Ellie that sat there at the kitchen table.

Dr. Michael told Ellie, "The day that you came to me, I held you in my arms. You were so weak and scared. I whispered over and over in your ear. . .Never look back. You're not going that way." Ellie seemed to understand. She nudged her nose under Dr. Michael's hand as he pet her. "Thank you," she said.

That night Ellie invited everyone that she could
think of to come to the barn for a meeting.

Ellie was surprised to see how many showed up. They wondered why "Ellie Ellie Big Fat Belly" gathered them there at the farm.

Ellie and Bonnie hopped up onto a haystack as Dr. Michael listened from afar. How proud he was of Ellie!

Ellie greeted her guests. "I've asked you to join me here to answer your question." "What question is that?" asked Wilbur the donkey. "Many of you wonder why it is that I don't seem to mind or get upset when you tease me. You wonder why I always smile and say 'Never Look Back'."

Ellie explained, "It's simple,
I've been taught that looking back
isn't always a good thing."

Dr. Michael turned down the lights in the barn. A hush filled the air. There in front of everyone, was a screen with the picture of Ellie on the day that she arrived at the farm.

"This was me, my friends. This was me on the day that Dr. Michael saved me." They all stared in shock as they looked from the screen to Ellie. "We are sorry Ellie."